6/12

D1123249

I SPEAK

JED HENRY

ABRAMS BOOKS FOR YOUNG READERS
NEW YORK

INOSAUR !

The illustrations in this book were made with
pen and ink and watercolor on paper.

Cataloging-in-Publication Data has been applied for
and may be obtained from the Library of Congress.

ISBN: 978-1-4197-0233-4

Text and illustrations copyright © 2012 Jed Henry

Book design by Chad W. Beckerman

Printed and bound in China
10 9 8 7 6 5 4 3 2 1

Abrams Books for Young Readers are available at special
discounts when purchased in quantity for premiums and
promotions as well as fundraising or educational use. Special
editions can also be created to specification. For details,
contact specialsales@abramsbooks.com or the address below.

ABRAMS
THE ART OF BOOKS SINCE 1949
115 West 18th Street
New York, NY 10011
www.abramsbooks.com

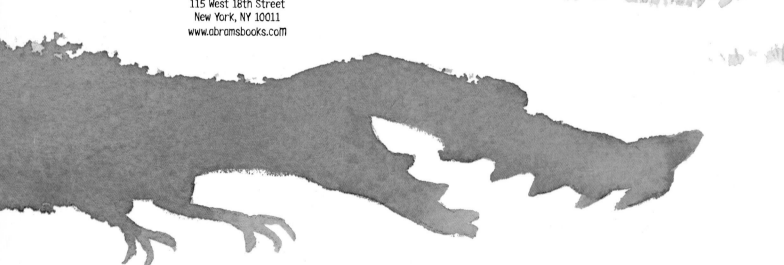

TO ALLOSAURUS FRAGILIS,
MY FAVORITE DINOSAUR. WE'RE TIGHT.
AND TO CHAD W. BECKERMAN,
WHO KNOWS HOW TO
SPEAK DINOSAUR.

Do you know how to speak Dinosaur?
I speak it all the time.

Dinosaurs don't ask,
"May I please play with you?"

They say,

GRIBBER, GRABBER,

GLOBBER, SLOBBER!

And dinosaurs like to shout,

BLE, BURPLE!

Dinosaurs never say, "Thank you."

They just say,

MUCKUS, BRUCKUS!

Dinosaurs don't say,
"I'm sorry," either.

Sometimes I speak Dinosaur to my mom.

When I do, she says, "No dinosaurs in the house." That's fine with me. Dinosaurs don't like being indoors anyway.

Speaking Dinosaur is fun, but it's kind of lonely sometimes. I wish I had some other dinosaurs to talk to.

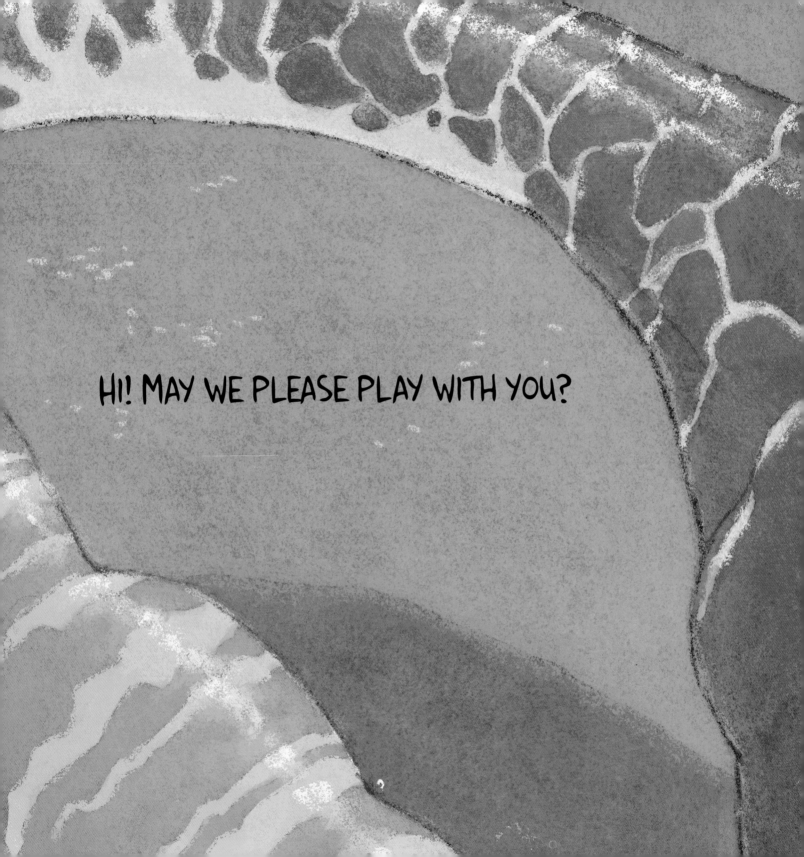

Dinosaurs ask, "MAY I?"
And dinosaurs say, "PLEASE"?

Sure, you can play with me.

THANK YOU!

You know how to speak Dinosaur, too!

GOO
GOO
GOO

May we please play outside a little longer?

Sure!

I speak Dinosaur!
Do you?